To my son, Jamari, my little
drummer boy, to my daughter,
Jamila, and to their mom, Annie.
Special thanks to my mom, who
watches over me from the Spirit
World, and to my dad, Roland Sr.,
for giving me the gift of music. To
all djembe players. Last, but not
least, thanks to Sandra Boyd
and Eboni, for bringing
Jamari's drum alive.
RJ

ILA HAU-NEE
EB

This book is dedicated to the
Toguna Cultural Center and to the
people who are helping to build
this dream one brick at a time.
"One finger cannot pick up
a stone."
BWD

Text copyright © 2004 by Eboni Bynum and Roland Jackson
Illustrations copyright © 2004 by Baba Wagué Diakité

Groundwood Books / Douglas & McIntyre
720 Bathurst Street, Suite 500, Toronto, Ontario M5S 2R4
Distributed in the USA by Publishers Group West
1700 Fourth Street, Berkeley, CA 94710

We acknowledge for their financial support the Government of Ontario through the
Ontario Media Development Corporation's Ontario Book Initiative.

National Library of Canada Cataloguing in Publication
Bynum, Eboni
Jamari's Drum / by Eboni Bynum and Roland Jackson;
with pictures on glazed tiles by Baba Wagué Diakité.
ISBN 0-88899-531-8
I. Jackson, Roland II. Diakité, Baba Wagué III. Title.
PZ7.B996Ja 2004   jC813'.6   C2003-907201-0

The illustrations are hand-painted ceramic tiles.
Printed and bound in China

JAMARI'S DRUM

by **Eboni Bynum** and **Roland Jackson**
with pictures on glazed tiles by
Baba Wagué Diakité

A Groundwood Book

Douglas & McIntyre

Toronto Vancouver Berkeley

JAMARI was a young man who lived in a village at the base of Chafua, a large mountain. When he was a child he played in the village square, keeping time to the

BEDE BADA BOOM KABEDE,
BEDE BADA BOOM KABEDE,
BEDE BADA BOOM KABEDE…

of Kubwa Chapa, the great village djembe drum. Baba Mdogo was the drummer.

Jamari was very curious and would often sit at Baba Mdogo's feet as he drummed. He loved the sound and the way the drum made the ground shake under him.

"Baba," Jamari would ask, "why do you play this drum every day? Don't you ever get tired?"

And Baba would laugh his great laugh. "Little one, I know this drum is only a musical instrument to you, but it is really the keeper of peace in our village. If I were to stop playing, the sky would turn black and the ground would grow hot and begin to melt beneath our feet."

With that Baba would close his eyes and beat the djembe a little faster.

BEDE BADA BOOM KABEDE,
BEDE BADA BOOM KABEDE,
BEDE BADA BOOM KABEDE...

Jamari knew there would be no more conversation today. He would return tomorrow with his questions.

Now Jamari had lived in the village of Opka his whole life. Rainy season and dry season came and went, each in its own time. Never did it so much as rain when it wasn't supposed to. Jamari could not even imagine such a calamity.

He asked his aunties. No, they had never witnessed any such thing. But then again, they couldn't remember a day without Baba Mdogo, either.

Then Jamari ran to his grandparents. No, they had never had one bad day in Opka. Everything had always happened as it should.

So Jamari shrugged off Baba's words and ran to play with his cousins.

As the years went by, Jamari grew strong and tall. Most of the elders, including his grandparents, had journeyed beyond the Great Divide. Soon only Baba Mdogo was left. There he sat on his stoop in the village square, beating his drum ceremoniously.

BEDE BADA BOOM KABEDE,
BEDE BADA BOOM KABEDE,
BEDE BADA BOOM KABEDE...

One day Jamari walked by Baba Mdogo on his way to the market

"Jambo, Baba!" he said.

"Jamari!" replied the great man, rising from his stoop.

Jamari didn't know what to think. He was almost old enough to be married and he had never seen Baba rise from that stoop before.

He rushed to Baba's side and marveled at just how small the old man actually was.

"I am the last of the original elders of Opka," said Baba. "Soon I, too, will make my journey. Someone will have to carry on the ways of our village and make sure the young ones don't forget them. For this I am turning to you. You are the only one who has ever taken any interest in this drum."

Jamari wasn't sure what the old man meant. The village was fine. The crops always grew tall and strong. The women wove beautiful cloth, which always fetched good prices during the festival. Everything was in harmony as it always had been.

But Jamari was a good man, as he had been a good boy, and he showed nothing but respect to his elders.

"What would you have me do, Baba?" Jamari asked.

Baba Mdogo put his hand upon Jamari's head, closed his eyes and said a couple of words. Then he picked up Kubwa Chapa and handed it to Jamari.

"You must beat this drum for Chafua every day, Jamari. The village depends on it." He pointed to the mountain. "Therein lies great danger to all that you know. Guard the village well. Play the djembe and peace will continue."

Jamari gazed up at the misty mountain in awe. He had always known Chafua. But it had never been more than a simple mountain to him.

He turned back to ask Baba what he meant, but the old man was gone. And so Jamari picked up Kubwa Chapa and continued on to the marketplace.

"Hmm," Jamari thought to himself. The disappearance of Baba Mdogo was very strange. But he vowed to keep his promise and he began to beat the drum as he walked.

BEDE BADA BOOM KABEDE,
BEDE BADA BOOM KABEDE,
BEDE BADA BOOM KABEDE...

A few more years came and went. Jamari began to court a young girl in the village. He was soon married, and with the responsibilities of being a father and keeping a good home, he forgot — some days — to beat the drum.

And gradually things began to change. There were no more elders to maintain the balance of old and new. So the new began to take over. And before long, Jamari had completely forgotten about Kubwa Chapa.

One day as Jamari tended the livestock, his wife and children came running.

"Jamari!" his wife screamed. "The world is coming to an end. The sky is turning black and the ground is growing hot beneath our feet. The rivers are bubbling and no one knows what to do."

Jamari rushed to the village square to see for himself. People were running wildly and yelling, "The sky is on fire! The mountain has gone mad!"

Jamari looked up. He couldn't believe his eyes. Gone was the blue sky. Huge rolling black clouds were turning day into night. Birds were falling to the ground. Jamari feared that the world was ending. He looked toward the mountain and saw a thin, glowing red line flowing down Chafua's side.

All at once Baba Mdogo's words came to mind. "The sky will turn black and the ground will grow hot and melt beneath your feet."

At once Jamari knew what to do. He ran back to his home calling, "Where is Kubwa Chapa? Has anyone seen my djembe?"

"It's in the shed," said Maku, Jamari's youngest child.

Jamari ran to the shed and found the djembe against the far wall. It was so long since he had played, he could barely remember what Baba Mdogo had taught him.

BEDE, BADA...BOOM
BEDE...BADA, BOOM, KABEDE...
BEDE.

But slowly, slowly it came back to him. Then he knew exactly what to beat.

BEDE BADA BOOM KABEDE,
BEDE BADA BOOM KABEDE,
BEDE BADA BOOM KABEDE...

He beat the djembe as he walked back to the village square.

"Turn back!" people cried out to him as they ran past. They thought he was foolish to go drumming into the night with heat and fire coming down the mountain.

BEDE BADA BOOM KABEDE,
BEDE BADA BOOM KABEDE,
BEDE BADA BOOM KABEDE...

But Jamari remembered Baba Mdogo's words. He knew it was his duty to save Opka. On he went, drumming.

When he reached the square, he sat down where he had seen Baba Mdogo sit so many times before. He sat and set a steady beat.

BEDE BADA BOOM KABEDE,
BEDE BADA BOOM KABEDE,
BEDE BADA BOOM KABEDE...

As villagers ran past him, Jamari saw that some were carrying crying children. Others tried to herd cattle that were mooing and bellowing and trying to run away. But he just sat and drummed. When his own wife begged him to stop and flee, Jamari drummed. Faster and faster he beat the djembe.

BEDE BADA BOOM KABEDE,
BEDE BADA BOOM KABEDE,
BEDE BADA BOOM KABEDE…

Jamari called silently to the elders to give him strength. The mountain rumbled and the ground began to shake. Jamari was frightened. Had he done something wrong?

But when he looked up at Chafua, he saw that the sky was beginning to clear.

He looked again. Was the lava actually flowing backward?

BEDE BADA BOOM KABEDE,
BEDE BADA BOOM KABEDE,
BEDE BADA BOOM KABEDE…

He beat the djembe in triumph and glee. He had done it. He had saved Opka. The villagers stopped running and made a circle around Jamari. They joined hands and danced a new ngoma.

Habari! Habari!
The gods have heard Jamari.
He is the champion of Kubwa Chapa.
He is the keeper of our peace.
Long live Jamari,
chosen by Baba Mdogo,
champion of Kubwa Chapa!

Peace and prosperity returned to Opka as quickly as they had been threatened. Never again did Jamari forget to beat the djembe. And to this day, you will find someone sitting in the square in Opka, beating the rhythm that calms mighty Chafua.

BEDE BADA BOOM KABEDE,
BEDE BADA BOOM KABEDE,
BEDE BADA BOOM KABEDE...

GLOSSARY OF SWAHILI WORDS

Baba Mdogo	Uncle
Chafua	Destruction
Djembe (jim-bay)	A handcarved wooden drum with a goatskin head.
Habari	News
Jambo	Hello
Kubwa Chapa	Big Beat
Ngoma	Drum dance